BLIZZARD!

A *SURVIVE!* Story

BY JAKE MADDOX

illustrated by Sean Tiffany

text by Marc Tyler Nobleman

Impact Books are published by Stone Arch Books,
A Capstone Imprint
151 Good Counsel Drive, P.O. Box 669
Mankato, Minnesota 56002
www.capstonepub.com

Library of Congress Cataloging-in-Publication Data
Maddox, Jake.
    Blizzard: A Survive! Story / by Jake Maddox; illustrated by Sean
Tiffany.
        p. cm. — (Impact Books. A Jake Maddox Sports Story)
        ISBN 978-1-4342-1206-1 (library binding)
        ISBN 978-1-4342-1397-6 (pbk.)
        [1. Blizzards—Fiction. 2. Survival—Fiction.] I. Tiffany, Sean, ill.
II. Title.
PZ7.M25643Bk 2009
[Fic]—dc222008031953

Summary:
They were supposed to be attending a volunteer dinner in their honor,
but instead, Owen and Gray have been stranded in the middle of a
raging blizzard. Once the storm subsides, the boys decide to try to
find their way back to civilization. But with no food or water, freezing
temperatures, and no help in sight, both boys begin to lose hope. Can
they make it safely home, or will the frozen elements become too much
for them to handle?

Creative Director: Heather Kindseth
Graphic Designer: Carla Zetina-Yglesias

Printed in the United States of America in Stevens Point, Wisconsin.
012010
005661R

TABLE OF CONTENTS

[Chapter 1]
OWEN

Two beads of sweat raced down the face of 16-year-old Owen Sevensky. He carried his suitcase across the airport parking lot.

His dad, Calvin, followed. Waves of heat floated up from the ground.

"Do you need help with that?" Calvin asked.

"No, I'm okay," Owen said. He wiped sweat from his face.

His corduroy pants, sweater, and coat made the hot Florida sun feel even hotter. He wished he were wearing a T-shirt and shorts like his dad was.

As they entered the airport, Owen let out a big sigh. "Air conditioning!" he said. "The greatest invention in human history."

"I'd say the best invention is airplanes," his dad said. "And yours is late."

Owen looked at the departures board. The takeoff time for Burlington, Vermont was an hour later than scheduled.

A TV nearby was showing a report about an October blizzard. The big snowstorm had just gone through northern New England.

"You'll like Vermont," Calvin said. "Even the outside is air-conditioned."

"More like deep frozen," Owen said. "If my flight is any later, I'll miss the whole thing." He pulled a piece of paper from his pocket and unfolded it. At the top, it read, "Extreme Community Service Awards Dinner for America's Teen Heroes."

Owen shook his head. "The dinner starts at 7 p.m.," he said. "I'm going to have to go there straight from the airport."

"Relax. The storm has to be affecting the other kids' flights too," Calvin said. "Since you have time to kill now, why don't you take off your coat and join me outside for a smoothie? It might be your last chance to see the sun for three days."

[Chapter 2]
GRAY

For most of the car ride, 16-year-old
Gray Tindle was silent. Then he snapped at
his sister, "Man, Becca, how can you stand
it so hot?" He reached over and turned
down the heat. His sister rolled her eyes.
Gray crossed his arms and put his head
back against the headrest.

"I know you're mad that you're going
on this trip instead of Caitlyn," Becca said.
"But it's what she wanted."

"No, what she wanted was to go herself," Gray said. "Then she had to get a bad cold."

"It's not like you don't deserve some pats on the back," Becca told him. "After all, you helped her with the community service. You should be proud. You should be happy you have the kind of girlfriend who would ask you to go to this special awards weekend in her place."

Gray stared out the window. A sign said they were a mile from the Indianapolis airport.

"Mostly I just hate wearing a suit," he admitted.

The news came on the radio. The first story was about a big blizzard that had just hit the northeastern United States.

"The worst is yet to come," the broadcaster said. "Another blizzard will move into the area later tonight."

"Sounds like you'll need to wear more than a suit," Becca said.

[Chapter 3]

STRANDED STRANGERS

Hours later, Owen waited for his suitcase in the busy Burlington International Airport. The room was packed.

People were stretched across chairs or sitting on the floor. Some were sleeping, using their bags as pillows. Some were just sitting there, looking uncomfortable.

On the departure screens, lists of flights were marked "canceled" in red letters.

When Owen looked out the window, he didn't see piles of snow. Instead, he saw plenty of concrete. "It doesn't seem so bad out there," he said to a woman standing next to him.

"This isn't the blizzard," the woman said. "It'll get worse later."

Finally, Owen saw his suitcase. He grabbed it. Then he headed outside. Even though he was wearing his winter coat and a thick sweater, he still felt the cold air. He shivered. Then he noticed that small snowflakes were starting to fall.

A car was supposed to pick him up and take him to the awards dinner. As he waited, he got colder and colder. After a few minutes, he opened his suitcase and pulled out another sweater.

He took off his winter coat. Then he put the second sweater over the one he was already wearing. Finally, he put the coat back on. He put on his hat, scarf, and gloves, too.

A guy his age was standing a few feet away. He looked at Owen and raised his eyebrows. "I'm not used to the cold," Owen explained. "I'm from Florida."

The other guy didn't say anything. He was wearing a warm coat, but no hat or gloves, and he had hair that went to his shoulders.

A minute later, a car pulled up. The sign in its window read "Extreme Community Service." The driver got out and put Owen's suitcase in the trunk. Owen got into the back seat. Then the guy with long hair got in.

"Oh, hi," Owen said. "You're going to the awards dinner too?"

The guy nodded.

"I'm Owen," Owen said.

"I'm Gray," the other guy said.

"My name's Jerry," the driver said from the front seat. "I'll get you there before the storm gets bad. You'll be eating in twenty minutes."

Owen smiled. "Great," he said.

"Where are you boys from?" Jerry asked.

"Florida," Owen told him.

"Indiana," Gray said.

"Well, you were lucky to make it," Jerry said. "Your flights were just about the last two in. They closed the airport about ten minutes ago."

Owen looked out the window. There were trees on both sides of the road. There were no houses, no signs, and no telephone poles.

"Uh oh," Jerry said. A car was stuck on the side of the road. A man was standing beside it, waving his arms.

Jerry stopped the car. He got out and walked over to the man.

"This guy is going to make us late," Owen said.

"So?" Gray said. "Are you actually excited about this dinner?"

"Well, yeah," Owen said. "Aren't you?"

"Not really," Gray admitted. "If you want to know the truth, I'm not even supposed to be here." He stared out the window at the snowflakes.

Jerry got back in the car. "I'm going to wait until his tow truck gets here," he said. "Don't worry. We'll still make it to the dinner on time."

A tow truck arrived in less than ten minutes. Another five minutes passed before it pulled the man's car out of a deep snowdrift. The snow was falling even more heavily. The man turned his car around and drove carefully down the hill.

The tow truck driver rolled down his window and Jerry rolled down his. "I'd head back too if I were you," the tow truck driver called.

Jerry said, "I'm not worried. I've got to get these guys where they're going." He waved and the tow truck drove off. Then Jerry tried to pull back on the road.

The rear tires spun. The car slid from side to side, but didn't move forward.

"That's not good," Jerry said. He looked over his shoulder. The tow truck was gone.

"We shouldn't have stopped," Owen mumbled.

"I can see why they chose you for a community service award," Gray said.

Owen frowned. "Whatever," he said.

Jerry opened his cell phone. "No signal," he said. "It worked outside — hold on." He got out of the car and went back to where he'd called the tow truck. Owen could see him shaking his head.

In a few seconds, Jerry walked back to the car. He brushed snow off his shoulders before getting in.

"I don't get it," he said. "It worked before. What about your phones?"

"My battery is dead," Owen said.

"I don't have a cell phone," Gray said.

Jerry sighed. "Well, we passed a gas station about a mile back," he said. "I'll go down there and bring help."

"That seems like a long way back," Owen said.

"It's really not far. It's no problem," Jerry said.

"What about us?" Gray asked.

"You'll be safer here," Jerry said. "Don't worry at all. I'll leave the car on, so you'll have heat. Keep a window open, just a crack, so you get fresh air. Don't try to move the car and do not get out."

"What should we do?" Owen asked.

"Just wait," Jerry said. "I'll be back soon. You'll only be a little late to your dinner."

Jerry smiled. Then he got out of the car. He vanished into the swirling snow.

Owen and Gray were silent. They watched the car windows become covered with snow. Soon, they couldn't see anything.

Chapter 4

RUNNING OUT

After ten silent minutes, Owen was bored. He tried to turn on his cell phone.

"I thought you said the batteries were dead," Gray said.

"They are," Owen said. "I was hoping it would work." He turned to look out the back window, but it was covered with snow. "Do you think Jerry made it yet?" he asked.

Gray shrugged. "Who knows," he said.

"Maybe we should go after him," Owen said. "Do you think we should?"

"No way," Gray said. "I'm staying right here. Jerry said he could handle it."

"The dinner already started," Owen said. "I know you don't care. But I do." He opened the door. "I'm going after him," Owen said. "Come with me if you want." He got out and shut the door.

For the first time that night, Gray felt afraid. He shut his eyes and tried to sleep.

* * *

Ten minutes later, the car door opened. Gray jumped. He even raised his fists, just in case.

"I couldn't get far," Owen said. He got into the car, bringing snow with him. "I couldn't even tell if I was still on the road."

Gray closed his eyes again. Owen did too. Soon, they were both asleep.

Later, Owen suddenly woke up. He looked at his watch. It was past 11 p.m. Panicked, he shook Gray awake.

"We fell asleep!" Owen shouted. "It's almost midnight." He elbowed the window and some of the snow slid off. Outside, it was still snowing. "I hope the driver's okay," Owen said.

Gray rubbed his eyes. "Do you have anything to eat?" he asked.

Owen raised his eyebrows. "Are you kidding? That's the first thought you have?"

"No," Gray said. "The first thought I had was that I'm glad we missed the dinner. Then I thought that you shouldn't freak out. 'I'm hungry' was my third thought."

Gray looked at the gas gauge. It was more than half empty. Then he said, "And my fourth thought is what we're going to do when we run out of gas, because I don't think anyone will find us tonight."

Owen frowned.

Gray went on, "I think we should stay in the car until the gas runs out or until morning, whichever comes first. Then we'll try to find help."

"You'll actually come with me this time?" Owen asked.

"Yes," Gray said. "But let's soak up as much heat as we can first. And seriously, do you have anything to eat?"

Owen looked through his backpack. "I have a few chocolate-covered raisins and an apple," he said.

Gray looked at the front seat. "We're in luck," he said. "Jerry had corn chips."

They ate for a while.

"We should save some," Owen said.

Gray laughed. He said, "Don't talk like a guy who doesn't think he'll be safe tomorrow."

"Whatever," Owen said. Then he stuffed the extra food in his pocket.

Chapter 5

OFF ROAD

"It's still snowing," Owen said, shaking Gray awake.

It was 7:30 a.m. The car was no longer running. It was very cold.

Gray tried to open his door, but it would barely budge. Snow was piled up past the window. "Whoa," he said.

"It's not as high on my side," Owen said. "Let's go." He shoved open his door and got out. Gray followed him outside.

Everything looked different in the daytime under several feet of heavy snow. Owen waded into snow up to his knees. He and Gray opened the car's trunk. They looked through their suitcases for warm clothes.

They got back in the car to bundle up.

"You need a hat," Owen said. "You lose the most heat through your head."

"I didn't bring one," Gray said.

"Then wrap a shirt or something around your head," Owen told him. "And something else around your neck, if you don't have a scarf."

When they were ready, they headed down the road. But after a few minutes, they were both exhausted. It was hard work wading through the tall piles of snow.

"Every kid in Florida is jealous of you northern kids and your snow days," Owen said. "Well, I'm not jealous anymore."

Gray smiled.

They walked through the falling snow for more than an hour. There was no sign of other human beings. Finally, they stopped.

Owen looked around. "I think this is the wrong way," he said.

"Are we still on the road?" Gray asked.

They looked around. It seemed like the trees were far enough apart for a road to pass through.

"I think so," Owen said. "I don't know. Do you remember if we've passed any streetlights?"

Gray thought for a moment. "No," he said.

Then he bent down and began to dig through the snow. When he reached the ground, it was soft and covered with leaves.

"No pavement," Gray said. He looked at Owen. "How could this happen?"

"It all looks the same," Owen said, shaking his head. "Let's go back to the car. This is stupid."

"Okay," Gray said. "Which way is that?"

They turned to look at their trail through the snow. "Hurry," Owen said. "The snow is covering our footprints really fast."

Quickly, they headed back along their own path. But soon they realized that the snow was falling faster than they could walk.

"Great," Owen said. "We're lost."

Gray tried to kick the snow, but he could barely move his foot because the snow was so deep.

Chapter 6

NEEDLES FOR NIGHT

"No one knows where we are," Owen said.

"Jerry does," Gray said.

Owen sighed. "No, he knows where we were," he said. "When we were in the car, where he told us to stay."

"We couldn't have walked far," Gray said. "We've got to be near something besides trees."

"I'm starting to get really cold," Owen admitted.

"You've got, like, two more layers on than me, and I'm fine," Gray said. "Come on. We can make it!"

Gray could hear Owen's teeth chattering. Gray was cold too, but he was mostly thirsty. He scooped up a handful of snow and ate it.

"You shouldn't do that," Owen said.

"Why? It wasn't yellow," Gray pointed out.

"Eating snow makes you even colder," Owen told him.

Just then, they heard a noise. It sounded like a helicopter. Then they saw something moving across the gray sky.

"Hey! Down here!" Owen yelled. They both screamed and waved their arms, but the helicopter didn't come any closer. A minute later, it was gone.

"At least we know someone is looking for us," Gray said.

Owen brushed the snow off a fallen tree trunk and sat down on it. Soon, flakes began to collect on his lap.

"I wish there was a way we could lie down or something. I need to rest," he said. "And eat."

"Don't we have some chips and raisins?" Gray asked.

"Just a few," Owen said. "Should we eat them now?"

"Might as well," Gray said. "We're hungry now, and we have to keep moving."

He paused. Then he went on, "I'm sure we'll find help soon. But no matter what, there's no way we can sleep out here."

"Gray," Owen said quietly, "I think we're going to have to."

Gray looked at the sky. The sun was sinking toward the west. It would get dark in just a few hours. He stood still. Then he nodded and said, "So we need a shelter."

Owen stood up. The two guys started walking, looking for a place that would work as somewhere to sleep.

Fifteen minutes later, they found a huge rock. It was at least twenty feet high. It looked like a small cliff.

One part of the rock stuck out. There was a patch of brown ground underneath, where snow couldn't reach.

"Here," Gray said. He hadn't said a word for several minutes. His mouth felt numb. It was hard to talk.

Owen stared nervously at the brown patch of ground. "I don't know," he said. "It doesn't look great."

"We don't have much time," Gray said. "This is the best thing we've found. Let's try to make this work. Let's find stuff to make it cozy."

"Like what?" Owen asked.

"I don't know," Gray said. "Branches, I guess. And anything else we can use to keep the snow and the wind out. Rocks, maybe. I don't know what else."

He looked around. Then he added, "Just don't go far. Make sure you can always see me and the cliff."

They both started to gather branches. No matter how many they found, it still seemed like they needed more. Gray stacked them up so that they made a wall.

Then Owen found a large fir tree with soft, long needles. The tree was about thirty feet from the rock.

"We can cover the ground with needles," Owen said. "Kind of like a bed."

"I don't know," Gray said. "It would be hard to carry the needles back. I don't know if it would be worth it."

"We need to protect ourselves from the ground," Owen said. "It's frozen. It'll freeze us." He thought for a moment, and then took off his coat.

"Dude, what are you doing?" Gray said. "Put your coat back on.

"I'll show you," Owen said. He laid his coat on the snow and used his hands to shovel needles onto it. Gray took off his coat too. They piled as many needles as they could onto their coats. Then they dragged the coats under the rock and spread the needles over the ground.

"I think this is great," Gray said, looking at what they'd done. "It's not a fancy hotel or anything, but it's better than freezing to death."

"That's for sure," Owen said. "Just in time, too," he added. The sun was sinking.

As Owen and Gray settled into their shelter, the snow stopped. Then the wind started.

Chapter 7

BEFORE THE ICE AGE

Owen and Gray stayed as far under the rocky overhang as they could. They kept their backs to the wind. They covered up with their coats and scarves.

Gray sat as close to Owen as he could, trying to stay warm. The needles didn't stop the cold coming from the ground as much as they had hoped. The wind whistled. Snow blew through holes in their branch wall.

"At least it hasn't fallen over yet," Gray said.

"I just wish we had found a cave," Owen said. "Even if we had to share it with a hibernating bear or something."

They gnawed on strips of bark. The bark tasted like a cereal box carton, but it helped them feel less hungry.

Owen and Gray were both tired, but the cold kept them awake. Neither of them felt like talking, but there was nothing else to do.

"Last night, what did you mean when you said you're not even supposed to be here?" Owen asked.

Gray hugged himself tightly, trying to stay warm. He tried to get a little more comfortable.

"My girlfriend is the one who deserved to be here," he said. "I don't mean here in the woods. I mean at the awards dinner. She's the community service champion. I was just helping because it made her happy. Plus, it meant we could spend more time together."

"So why isn't she here?" Owen asked.

"She got a cold," Gray said. They both laughed. Then Gray asked, "What about you? Why is this awards dinner so important to you?"

"Well, I'm not an athlete," Owen said. "Or an artist. I don't have a girlfriend. But it doesn't take any skill to do community service. Anyone can pick up trash in the park and along the highway."

"Is that what you did?" Gray asked.

"Yeah," Owen said. "For twelve hours straight." He held up two gloved fingers. "Two days in a row."

"Are you serious?" Gray asked. "No breaks?"

"I stopped to eat a sandwich for lunch and dinner and made a couple runs to the bathroom," Owen told him. "But otherwise, no breaks. I even got on the news."

"Wow," Gray said.

"Go on. Say it," Owen said. "I know. I need to get a life."

"No, I wasn't going to say that," Gray said. "It's really cool. Really. I don't care that much about anything."

"You gave up a long weekend to fly here for someone else," Owen pointed out. "That's caring."

"Okay," Gray said. "Well, I don't have patience like you do, I guess."

"We both have more patience than we thought we did a day ago," Owen said. "I just hope it lasts through the night."

Chapter 8

COLD SNAPS

In the middle of the night, Owen and Gray woke up when they heard something snap. Then they heard a loud crash. Their wall had blown over. They couldn't see it, but they could feel the blast of icy air.

They were too cold to get up to fix the wall. Side by side, they curled up as closely as they could. Then they tried to forget where they were. Somehow, they both fell asleep again.

In the morning, Owen opened his eyes. He was shocked to see a clear sky.

His feet felt tingly, and he couldn't feel his ears at all. He also couldn't stop shivering.

A few minutes later, Gray woke up. "I'm so thirsty," he said.

"Let's get out of here," Owen said. "Moving around will help get our blood flowing. That'll warm us up a little. And maybe we'll be able to find some water somewhere."

"You sure I can't just eat some snow?" Gray asked.

Owen rolled his eyes, but then he realized that Gray was joking. "Not unless you melt it first," Owen said.

"I forgot my microwave," Gray replied.

Owen smiled, but his mouth felt locked by the cold.

The two started walking. Owen had a hard time standing. Sometimes he fell down, landing on his knees in the snow. Whenever he fell, Gray helped him up.

Sometime before noon, they came to the top of a hill. The forest was silent, except for a sound off in the distance.

"Is that what I think it is?" Gray asked.

"I don't know," Owen said. "We could be dreaming."

"Let's find out," Gray told him. They hurried, rushing in the direction of the sound. Soon, they were standing near a stream.

"This is great," Owen said.

They bent down. Both of them took off their gloves and slurped water from their cupped hands.

The water wasn't as cold as the snow, but it was cold enough to hurt their throats. It was worth it. Owen thought it was the best drink of water he had ever had.

Gray stood up and peered down the hill, following the stream.

"Let's go that way," he said, pointing. "I think there's a clearing down there. There might be a house, or a building, or something."

"Okay," Owen said.

They made their way down the hill. When they were about halfway down, Owen fell down into the snow. Gray pulled him up.

"I can't keep going right now," Owen said. "You go. I'll catch up."

"You aren't allowed to say you can't do something," Gray said. "You're the one who spent a whole weekend picking up bottles and newspapers. Besides, I'm not leaving you all alone out here."

"You have to leave me here," Owen said. "I'm too cold to move."

"If you're too cold, you have to move," Gray told him. "Come on."

Owen didn't move.

"Come on, Owen. You're the king of community service," Gray said. "Right now, the only community you've got is me. And I need your help. You think you can't go on, but I can't leave without you. You have to try."

Slowly, Owen stood up. He took a step forward. Three steps later, they saw that Gray had been right. There was a clearing at the bottom of the hill.

"I hope there's something there," Gray said. He and Owen tried to hurry the rest of the way down the hill. But when they reached the clearing, they stopped and stared. There was no building. No house. Nothing. Just the clearing, and then more trees and snow.

Owen felt like crying.

"No, it's still good," Gray told him. "I'll make an SOS."

Owen leaned against a tree. He watched as Gray headed into the clearing and began to walk around. It was funny to watch.

Gray walked back and forth. Sometimes he jumped. When he reached the other end of the clearing, he made a final leap. Then he turned and faced Owen.

"What do you think?" Gray yelled.

Just then, they heard a loud crack. Owen realized what it was before Gray did.

Owen yelled, "Gray! It's not a clearing! It's a lake!"

Gray began to run. Then they heard a louder crack. Behind Gray, a chunk of ice fell into the water.

"Don't run!" Owen yelled. "Crawl!"

Gray looked scared, but he did what Owen said. He lay down in the snow and started to move on his hands and feet over the ice. The ice made creaky noises below him.

Finally, Gray reached the bottom of the hill. Then he stood up and carefully walked over to Owen.

"I can't believe I made it," Gray said.

"I can't believe it either," Owen said. His heart was pounding. "I'm glad you're okay," he added.

"It was that last jump that did it," Gray said. "The dot of the exclamation point." He pointed at the lake. "Take a look," he said.

"I can't see anything," Owen said.

They walked up the hill a few feet. "Can you see it now?" Gray asked.

Owen looked at the lake. He could see that Gray had stamped "HELP!" into the snow.

"That's awesome," Owen said. "Good thinking." He paused. Then he asked, "So, now what do we do?"

Gray pointed to a fir tree. It was so large that a patch of ground underneath it was still brown, not covered with snow. "Let's sit under there and wait," Gray said. "We can pray for a helicopter or an angel or anything else that can fly us out of here."

Chapter 9

UP AND OUT

The two sat down under the tree.
They sat back to back, trying to get more
warmth.

"After all that," Gray said, "do you think
the HELP can even be seen from the sky?"

Owen nodded. "Yeah, I do," he said.
"You did a great job."

Moments later, he fell asleep. Not long
after that, Gray did too.

After a while, they were awakened by a motor. Gray jumped up. There was a helicopter overhead, hovering just above the trees.

"Hey! Over here!" Gray yelled. He waved his arms around and screamed, but his voice was too weak to be heard. Then he made snowballs and hurled them in the air.

Owen woke up. He tried to help Gray, but he couldn't shout. He could hardly stand.

Suddenly, the helicopter started to sink down toward the ground. Gray and Owen watched as a cable ladder was thrown out. The ladder hit the snow several hundred feet away. It stretched back up to the helicopter.

The helicopter's spinning blades made the snow blow like crazy. Gray and Owen slowly pushed their way through the snow to the ladder.

A woman in rescue gear was climbing down. She smiled when she saw Gray and Owen. "You're alive!" she said.

"He's really weak," Gray shouted over the noise from the helicopter. Owen's eyes kept closing.

"What about you?" the woman shouted.

"I can hold on," Gray shouted back.

The woman attached a harness to Owen. Then she spoke into the headset she was wearing.

Gray held on tight to the ladder. Soon, it began to rise, slowly pulling up all three people.

From the air, Gray could see that there were no buildings for miles.

The helicopter brought Gray and Owen to a hospital. A nurse called their parents. Owen and Gray were given lukewarm baths.

Afterward, they wrapped up in thick blankets and sipped broth. The nurses said that if they had too much food too fast, it would hurt their bodies.

A doctor checked both of them. When he was done, he said that neither of them had any frostbite. "However," he said, "one more night out there and you could have lost your foot, or your fingers."

After the doctor left, another man came into the room. It was Jerry, the driver from the airport. He looked tired and worried.

"I'm so sorry," Jerry said. "I tried to send help the night of the storm. But the road was closed. No one could get through. They finally opened it late the next morning. But you were gone when we made it to the car."

"We figured that's what happened," Owen said. "Don't worry. It's not your fault."

"I'm just so relieved you're okay," Jerry said.

"Me too. But mostly, I'm relieved I didn't have to wear a suit," Gray said. He and Owen looked at each other and smiled.

ABOUT THE AUTHOR

Marc Tyler Nobleman has written books on everything from ghosts to Groundhog Day, belly flops to the Battle of the Little Bighorn, Superman to summertime activities. Besides writing books, he is also a cartoonist whose work has appeared in more than 100 magazines. He has never been through a real disaster but is living proof that it is possible to survive a bad hairdo.

ABOUT THE ILLUSTRATOR

When Sean Tiffany was growing up, he lived on a small island off the coast of Maine. Every day, from sixth grade until he graduated from high school, he had to take a boat to get to school. When Sean isn't working on his art, he works on a multimedia project called "OilCan Drive," which combines music and art. He has a pet cactus named Jim.

GLOSSARY

blizzard (BLIZ-urd)—a heavy snowstorm

canceled (KAN-suhld)—if something is canceled, it will not happen as planned

clearing (KLEER-ing)—an area of woods from which trees have been removed

community service (kuh-MYOO-nuh-tee SUR-viss)—work that helps a community, or group of people

departures (di-PAR-churz)—at an airport, the planes that are leaving

exhausted (eg-ZAWST-id)—very tired

overhang (OH-vur-hang)—a part of something that sticks out

patience (PAY-shuhnss)—if you have patience, you can put up with problems or delays without getting angry or upset

shelter (SHEL-tur)—a place where you can keep covered in bad weather

skill (SKIL)—the ability to do something well

vanished (VAN-ishd)—disappeared suddenly

BIG BLIZZARDS

The wind and snow of a big blizzard can cause widespread damage. These storms left their mark.

The Great White Hurricane (March 1888): Snowdrifts reached heights of nearly 50 feet (15 meters) during this New England storm. More than 400 people died.

The Chicago Blizzard of 1967: As 23 inches (58.4 centimeters) of snow fell, drivers left 50,000 cars and 800 buses scattered on roadways. 650 students were stuck spending the night at their schools. Surprisingly, just two days before the storm, the temperature was 65 degrees Fahrenheit (18 degrees Celsius).

Storm of the Century (March 1993): Twenty-six states were affected by this three-day storm. More than 40 inches (101 centimeters) of snow fell in some areas. In the end, it caused more than $3 billion in damage.

SURVIVAL TIPS

If you're stuck in a car during a blizzard, what should you do?

- For heat, run the engine for ten minutes every hour.

- Open a window slightly for fresh air.

- Move your hands and legs around to keep blood moving in your body.

- Tie a bright cloth to the car door to alert passersby that you need help.

DISCUSSION QUESTIONS

1. Gray and Owen are both being honored for community service. What are some kinds of community service that would help your community?

2. What are some things that would be helpful to have if you were stranded in a blizzard?

3. Do you think Owen and Gray did the right thing when they left the car to try to find help? Why or why not? What do you think they should have done?

WRITING PROMPTS

1. What do you think would have happened if Gray and Owen hadn't left the car? Write a story in which the boys decide not to leave the car.

2. If you were stranded in a blizzard, who would you want to be with? Write about that person.

3. On page 30, Owen says that kids in Florida are jealous of kids who live in the northern United States and get lots of snow. Choose a place that has a different climate from where you live. What would you enjoy about the different weather? What wouldn't you enjoy? Write about it.

INTERNET SITES

Do you want to know more about subjects related to this book? Or are you interested in learning about other topics? Then check out FactHound, a fun, easy way to find Internet sites.

Our investigative staff has already sniffed out great sites for you!

Here's how to use FactHound:

1. Visit *www.facthound.com*

2. Select your grade level.

3. To learn more about subjects related to this book, type in the book's ISBN number: **9781434212061**.

4. Click the **Fetch It** button.

FactHound will fetch the best Internet sites for you!